Dear Fred

To Besha, Fred, Grace and Ruby
– S.R.

To Greer
– K.G.

Viking
Penguin Books Australia Ltd
487 Maroondah Highway, PO Box 257
Ringwood, Victoria 3134, Australia
Penguin Books Ltd, Harmondsworth, Middlesex, England
Viking Penguin, A Division of Penguin Books USA Inc.
375 Hudson Street, New York, New York 10014, USA
Penguin Books Canada Limited
10 Alcorn Avenue, Toronto, Ontario, Canada M4V 3B2
Penguin Books (N.Z.) Ltd
182-190 Wairau Road, Auckland 10, New Zealand

First published by Penguin Books Australia, 1994
1 3 5 7 9 10 8 6 4 2
Copyright © Susanna Rodell, 1994
Illustrations Copyright © Kim Gamble, 1994

Typeset in Bembo

Made and printed in Australia by Southbank Book

National Library of Australia
Cataloguing in Publication data:

Rodell, Susanna.
Dear Fred.

ISBN 0 670 85493 X.

I. Gamble, Kim. II. Title.

A 823.3

The illustrations in this book are executed
in watercolour on Arches paper. Book designed
by Cathy van Ee.

Dear Fred

Susanna Rodell
Illustrated by
Kim Gamble

VIKING

Dear Fred,
I am still missing you.

When we went away, I didn't know it would
be this long. Mummy says it's been almost a year.
It feels funny that you're not here. Mummy says
you're still my brother and you will always be
my brother, even though you're far away.

She says she misses you, too. She says that's the kind of thing that happens in complicated families like ours.

I like my school here in America. I have two
new friends, Jessica and Jacob. They come to
my house to play.

I remember, back home in Australia, when
it was our turn to have you at our house, we
used to play every day after school. It was
good playing with you. The weeks you were
with your papa, I always missed you. Nobody
else had time to play with me.

I liked it when we played knights and
dragons. You always let me be the Queen

and you would be my knight. I got to order
you around and you called me Your Majesty.

My favourite was when we made mud
banquets on your stove in the back yard.
You were such a good cook. We made big
stews and you let me stir them. We put in
ashes from the barbecue, and grass and berries.

We made beautiful cakes and decorated
them with fuchsia flowers and pretty leaves.
We made mud tea and everybody would
come out and pretend to eat.

We don't have a back yard here.

Sometimes you got angry at me.

I was little and you said everyone
thought I was the cute one and you
were just a kid. You got in trouble if
I cried. You said it wasn't fair.

Well, now Ruby's the cute one and
everybody's always going all googly-woogly
over her, and I'm just a kid.

She's just learned how to walk.
I've known how to walk for ages.

Sometimes Ruby eats my crayons.

Once I saved her life in the bath.
She fell over and her face was in the
water and I pulled her up.

Mummy says I'm a good big sister,
but it's hard looking after her all by myself.

I wish you were here to help.

Mummy says you'll come over at Christmas time. I can't wait. We could go skating and build a snowman.

Ruby's okay, really.
I reckon you'd like her. She's very soft.

I'm bigger now. When you come
to visit, I promise I won't cry.

If you get in trouble, I'll get in
trouble, too. It'll be fair.

Mummy wrote this letter down for me.
I told her what to say.

I love you, Freddy,
and I hope you remember me.

Love, Grace . . .